With much love to my little brother Dougal,
or fabulous Flapdougal as I shall call him from now on –
CS

With love to Mum and Dad Twomey
for their amazing support and
constant encouragement –
EG

First published in 2011 by Scholastic Children's Books
Euston House, 24 Eversholt Street
London NW1 1DB
a division of Scholastic Ltd
www.scholastic.co.uk
London ~ New York ~ Toronto ~ Sydney ~ Auckland
Mexico City ~ New Delhi ~ Hong Kong

Text copyright © 2011 Chae Strathie
Illustrations copyright © 2011 Emily Golden

PB ISBN 978 1407 110 837

The Fabulous Flapdoodles

SCHOLASTIC

When stars fill the sky at the end of the day,
the **Fabulous Flapdoodles**
come out to play.

They wait in the darkness for soft, sleepy snores,
Then slip through your windows and under your doors.

They're brimful of magic
and mischievous tricks,
And zoom round your room
upon brooms built for six.

They've got stripey red stockings

and wild purple hair,

They're as small as a mouse

but as strong as a bear.

They'll juggle your wardrobe while dancing a jig,
But even a flea wouldn't say they were big.

They always have things hidden under their hats,
Like cookies and spell books and tiny green cats.
They've pockets and lockets and satchels and sacks,
And big shiny starwhizzers strapped to their backs.

For giggles they jiggle
the hands on your clocks,

And hide single socks
in their **Flapdoodle** box

But though they might doodle
and draw on your wall,
They don't just make mischief –
oh no, not at all!

They like to make sure that you don't get a fright
From all of the things that go
"BUMP!" in the night,

Like **big scary hairies** from under the bed,

And **small hairy scaries**
with more than one head.

Those **Boggle-eyed Bugwaggles** don't stand a chance

If caught in the glare of a **Flapdoodle** trance.

And grumpy blue **Bumpalumps** aren't quite so tough

When blown out the door with an effortless puff.

They have nets made of moonbeams to trap **naughty ghouls**

And practical jokes to make **ghosts** look like fools.

They're always on duty when
you have a snooze,
To shield you from showers
of **bogeymens'** ooze.

And **giants** won't enter
your bedroom at all,

For fear they'll be shrunk
till they're two inches tall.

From slithery **Snarkles** to **Weezers** with wings,
The Flapdoodles terrify terrible things.

When masses of **monsters** leap out at one time,
All **stumpy** and **stompy** and **covered in slime,**

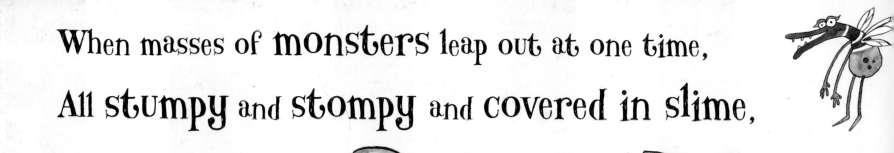

These miniature marvels
put up such a fight,
They send them all scampering
into the night.

And when their task's over and day starts to break,
The Flapdoodles vanish before you awake.

But though you won't see them they'll always be there,
To stop you from getting a toe-curling scare.

They hide out of sight behind clouds in the sky
With long golden telescopes held to their eye,
Waiting and watching to make sure you're good,
And settle down gently to sleep when you should.